Dear Parent:

Congratulations! Your child is taking the first steps on an exciting journey. The destination? Independent reading!

STEP INTO READING® will help your child get there. The program offers five steps to reading success. Each step includes fun stories and colorful art. There are also Step into Reading Sticker Books, Step into Reading Math Readers, Step into Reading Phonics Readers, Step into Reading Write-In Readers, and Step into Reading Phonics Boxed Sets—a complete literacy program with something to interest every child.

Learning to Read, Step by Step!

Ready to Read **Preschool–Kindergarten**
• big type and easy words • rhyme and rhythm • picture clues
For children who know the alphabet and are eager to begin reading.

Reading with Help **Preschool–Grade 1**
• basic vocabulary • short sentences • simple stories
For children who recognize familiar words and sound out new words with help.

Reading on Your Own **Grades 1–3**
• engaging characters • easy-to-follow plots • popular topics
For children who are ready to read on their own.

Reading Paragraphs **Grades 2–3**
• challenging vocabulary • short paragraphs • exciting stories
For newly independent readers who read simple sentences with confidence.

Ready for Chapters **Grades 2–4**
• chapters • longer paragraphs • full-color art
For children who want to take the plunge into chapter books but still like colorful pictures.

STEP INTO READING® is designed to give every child a successful reading experience. The grade levels are only guides. Children can progress through the steps at their own speed, developing confidence in their reading, no matter what their grade.

Remember, a lifetime love of reading starts with a single step!

 Published in the United States by Random House Children's Books, a division of Random House, Inc., 1745 Broadway, New York, NY 10019, and in Canada by Random House of Canada Limited, Toronto, in conjunction with Disney Enterprises, Inc.

Visit us on the Web!
www.stepintoreading.com
www.randomhouse.com/kids
Educators and librarians, for a variety of teaching tools, visit us at
www.randomhouse.com/teachers

Library of Congress Cataloging-in-Publication Data
Lagonegro, Melissa.
Vidia takes charge / by Melissa Lagonegro ; illustrated by the Disney Storybook Artists.
p. cm.
ISBN 978-0-7364-2686-2 (trade) — ISBN 978-0-7364-8086-4 (lib. bdg.)
I. Disney Storybook Artists. II. Tinkerbell (Motion picture) III. Title.
PZ7.L14317Vi 2010 [E]—dc22 2009053330

Printed in the United States of America 10 9 8 7 6 5 4 3

STEP INTO READING®

Vidia Takes Charge

By Melissa Lagonegro
Illustrated by
the Disney Storybook Artists

Random House New York

Tinker Bell and her friends
are bringing summer
to the mainland!

Terence and Tinker Bell fly
to fairy camp.
This is where the fairies
prepare for summer.

One fairy paints lovely lines
on a butterfly's wings.
Other fairies teach crickets to sing.
Everyone is very busy!

Suddenly, humans drive by.
The fairies hide so the humans
cannot see them.
But Tinker Bell is curious.
She follows the humans' car.
Vidia is a fast-flying fairy.
She speeds after Tink
and tries to stop her.

Tink peers at the humans.

They get out of the car.

A little girl named Lizzy skips
into the house.

Her father carries their luggage.

Tink wants to look
at the car.
She flies into the engine.
"Vidia, this is amazing,"
says Tink.
But Vidia is angry.

"You shouldn't be this close!"
she yells.
Tink is too busy to listen.
She pulls a lever.
Water sprays out at Vidia.
Now Vidia is angry and wet.

Soon, the humans come back.
Tink and Vidia quickly hide.
Lizzy and her father
catch a butterfly.
They look at its pretty wings.
Lizzy believes that fairies
painted them.

But her father does not believe
in fairies.
"Fairies are not real,"
he tells Lizzy.

Tink and Vidia try to leave.

But Vidia can't fly.

Her wings are still wet.

Tink tells Vidia she's sorry.

Vidia just yells at Tink.

But Tink isn't listening.
She sees a fairy house
that Lizzy made.
"Wow!" says Tink.

Tink goes into the house.

She starts to explore.

"We're not supposed

to go near human houses!"

warns Vidia.

But Tink won't listen.

Vidia decides to teach
Tink a lesson.
She makes a great gust of wind
slam the door shut.
Now Tink is locked
inside the fairy house!

Lizzy catches Tink.

She puts Tink in a birdcage

so the cat cannot reach her.

Vidia watches from the window.

She did not mean

for Tink to get caught!

Vidia rushes back to fairy camp.
She tells the other fairies that
Tink is trapped.
"We have to hurry and save her!"
cries Vidia.
But a storm has begun.
The fairies cannot fly
in the rain.
Clank and Bobble have an idea.
"We're going to build a boat,"
they tell everyone.

At Lizzy's house,
Tink is scared.
But Lizzy does not want
to hurt Tink.

Lizzy shows Tink
her fairy drawings.
Tink realizes how much
Lizzy loves fairies.

Lizzy's father hears Lizzy
talking to Tink.
He goes to her room.
But Lizzy wants
to keep Tink a secret.
She hides Tink
until her father leaves.

Tinker Bell is ready to leave.

Lizzie wants her to stay.

“There’s so much we can do,”

pleads Lizzie.

Tink teaches Lizzy
about fairies.
Lizzy takes notes.
Tink helps Lizzy paste them
in her journal.

Meanwhile,

Vidia and the other fairies

sail to Tink.

Their rescue boat goes

over a waterfall!

Silvermist makes a water slide

to keep the fairies safe.

Soon, Tinker Bell leaves.
She looks in the window
and sees Lizzy.

Lizzy wants to show her father
the fairy journal.
But her father does not
have time for her.
He is too busy fixing leaks.

Tink decides to stay
with Lizzy a little longer.
Lizzy is very happy.

That night,
the rescue team gets
in more trouble!
Vidia is stuck
in the mud.
The other fairies try
to help her.
But a car is coming!

Iridessa makes the driver stop
and get out of the car.
The fairies grab his shoelace.
The shoelace pulls them
out of the mud!

Tink wants to help
Lizzy and her father.
She tinkers with the leak
in their house.
She fixes it!

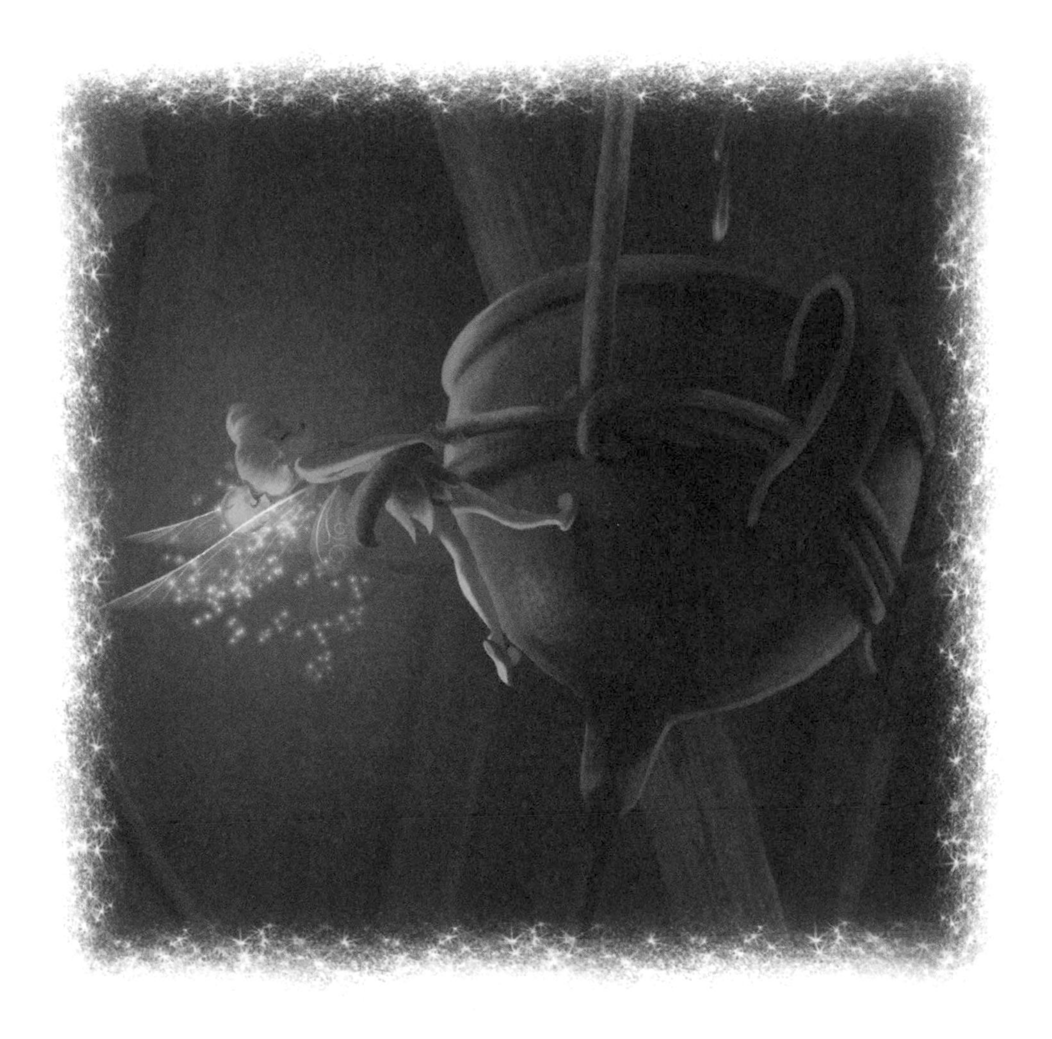

Tink sees a butterfly
in the office.
Lizzy's father trapped it
in a jar to study it.
Tink decides to set
the butterfly free.

Lizzy's father is very angry
that his butterfly is gone.
He blames Lizzy.

Meanwhile,
Vidia tells the other fairies
that she trapped Tink
in the fairy house.
"This is not your fault,"
says Rosetta.
The fairies vow to work together
to find Tink.

Tink sprinkles Lizzy
with pixie dust
to cheer her up.
Lizzy flies!

The rescue team arrives.
Lizzy's cat corners them.
The fairies distract the cat
while Vidia looks for Tink.

Lizzy's father goes

to Lizzy's room.

Tink flies up to him.

She proves that fairies are real.

Lizzy's father is shocked!

He tries to catch Tink.

Vidia arrives just in time.

She pushes Tink

out of the way.

But Lizzy's father

catches Vidia instead!

Lizzy begs her father
to let Vidia go.
But he refuses.
Now Tink must rescue Vidia!

The other fairies agree to help.

Lizzy wants to help, too.

The fairies sprinkle Lizzy

with pixie dust.

"All aboard!"

Tink tells the fairies.

Lizzy and the fairies
find Lizzy's father.
He can't believe that
Lizzy is flying!
"It has to be magic," he says.
"It is," says Lizzy. "Fairies!"
Lizzy's father believes her.
And he finally believes
in fairies.
He lets Vidia go.

The next day,
the fairies have a tea party
with Lizzy and her father.
Lizzy pours tea.
The fairies bring flowers.

The fairies watch

Lizzy and her father

read together.

Tink smiles.

Her tinkering has fixed a leak

and a family!